S0-ALN-773

# COMPUTER OVERBYTE

## PLUS TWO MORE CODEBREAKERS

By Andrew Bromberg

Illustrated by Mary Kornblum

Greenwillow Books • New York

From a concept by Edward D. Brown.

Copyright © 1982 by William Morrow and Company, Inc. All rights reserved. No part of this book may be reproduced or utilized in any form or by any means, electronic or mechanical, including photocopying, recording or by any information storage and retrieval system, without permission in writing from the Publisher, Greenwillow Books, a division of William Morrow & Company, Inc., 105 Madison Avenue, New York, N.Y. 10016.

Library of Congress catalog number 82-081248

Printed in the United States of America. First Edition. 1 2 3 4 5 6 7 8 9 10

# Contents

# INTRODUCTION

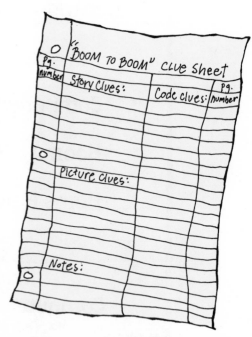

This book contains three mystery stories. But these are no ordinary mysteries that you just sit back and read. Each story contains a mystery to solve and a code to break. Go through the stories carefully, paying close attention to note any possible clues that might be hidden in either the stories or the pictures. Make a clue sheet like the one shown. On one side, jot down all the facts and observations that will lead you to the culprit and, on the other side, all the clues that will help you break the code. Then read over your notes. Try to come up with your own solutions before looking up Amanda's and Sherlock's solutions in the back of the book.

*Some Hints*

The stories and pictures work very closely together. Sometimes a clue may be found in the story and then show up in the picture. Sometimes a clue may show up only in the picture or only in the story. Besides checking the story with the picture, you may also want to check pictures that appear early in the story with the pictures that appear later on. Comparing pictures might give you a clue that you might not otherwise detect. Get to know all the little facts, places and objects. If you think you're ready, turn the page and begin!

# COMPUTER OVERBYTE

"I just can't figure out where I went wrong," Amanda complained. "I choreographed the dance, then I programmed the choreography, but if we follow the printout, everyone's going to be falling on top of everyone else."

Sherlock flipped the pages of computer printout back and forth. "I don't know what's wrong, Amanda.

I'll have to study it more carefully when we get home. But what's this page attached to your program?" Amanda leaned across the cafeteria table to see better. "I don't know. Someone must have forgotten it."

"Looks like a payment record," Sherlock observed. "No code though, so we can't figure out who to give it back to."

"Well, who cares, anyway?" Amanda said. "It's *my* program I'm worried about."

"Shh!" At the other end of the table, Amy Stone looked up from her chess game with Tommy Wolfe and glared at them.

"Those two are really impossible," Amanda whispered just loud enough for the chess players to hear. "Come on, let's go outside."

"Actually," Sherlock said when they were outside in the hall, "that printout reminded me that I have to use the computer myself. I've got some payments to make for the Athletic Club's road trip next week. That electronic transfer system the school set up really makes it easy."

"It seems to me that being treasurer of that club is really keeping you busy," Amanda commented. "But, okay, I'll meet you at the bike rack after school."

Sherlock sat down in front of the terminal and punched some buttons. The screen lit up, and he entered his first payment. Instead of the usual polite acknowledgment, the terminal was flashing a rejection. Sherlock couldn't believe his eyes. He tried again and got the same response.

"It's not possible," Sherlock said out loud to the flashing terminal. "I know there's much more than thirty-five dollars in that account." Too angry to try again, he logged off and stomped out of the room.

"I just don't understand," he was complaining to Amanda as they pedaled home. "I know I haven't overdrawn the account. I've been very careful."

"Well," said Amanda, "you keep written records at home, don't you? You'll just have to go through them to be sure you did the arithmetic correctly."

But Sherlock checked everything twice and got the same answer both times. There should have been $135.27 in the Athletic Club account.

"What am I going to tell the guys in the club?" he asked, moaning. "If I don't pay these bills, we're not going to be able to go on the trip. They're going to kill me!"

Amanda was puzzled, too. "Well, we're just going to have to figure it out then. The school computer's hooked up directly to the bank, isn't it?" she asked.

"Sure, you know that. Each of the club treasurers has a code — like mine's LOCK. We enter the payments we want to make, and the bank transfers the money directly. It's foolproof."

"Well, obviously not quite foolproof," Amanda replied. "Tomorrow we'll just have to get to school early so you can call up the bank records on the terminal. Maybe you forgot to write down one of the payments you made. You can check the computer's records against your own, and if there's an error you ought to find it that way."

Sherlock was still dubious. "Honestly, Amanda, I don't think I made a mistake, but I guess checking the records on the computer is the only way to prove it."

"Good. Now that we've settled your problem, maybe you can help me get the bugs out of my choreography program."

"I wouldn't call it settled exactly, but I can't do anything more about it now. So let's see if we can solve your problem."

They huddled together over the sheets of computer printout.

"There! I think that does it," Amanda sighed, a couple of hours later. "I'll run it again tomorrow to be sure."

Amanda and Sherlock were not the first to arrive at school the next morning. Some members of the Drama Club were already rehearsing in the auditorium, and Tommy Wolfe was holding a meeting of the Chess Club in one of the empty classrooms.

"I heard the Chess Club's really having a hard time raising money this year," Sherlock commented as they passed the open classroom door.

Luckily, no one was using the terminal. Sherlock logged in his code and punched in the commands that

would call up his payment records for the last month.

"I don't believe it! Look at that," Sherlock exclaimed. "I never made a payment like that."

"Well, someone did," said Amanda. "And that's a very strange code. Everyone I know in computer class uses a part of their name, like we do."

"I just can't believe it," Sherlock repeated. "Someone's got hold of my access code and is taking money out of the Athletic Club account. We've actually got an embezzler in the school!"

"And the only way to discover who it is, is to find out who's using that code. Let's look at the class list for our computer course. Maybe someone's using initials or something like that."

But just then the first-period bell rang, and Amanda and Sherlock had to hurry to their classes.

"I'll meet you in the cafeteria," Sherlock called to his sister, as they grabbed their books and rushed off in opposite directions.

At lunch, they both gobbled their sandwiches so that they'd have time enough to study the list of names before the bell rang again. The classroom was empty, and the list was thumbtacked to the wall behind the teacher's desk. Sherlock read the names out loud while Amanda peered over his shoulder.

"Well, I don't think it could be any of these," he said finally.

"Neither do I," said Amanda. "There are only four last names beginning with K — Kane, Kessler, King, and Krauss — and none of them has a first name beginning with P."

Sherlock slumped against the wall. "That does it, then. I don't see how we're ever going to find the embezzler. I'm just going to have to confess. I'll call a club meeting and tell them the trip will have to be cancelled. I'll explain about the embezzler. Maybe they won't kill me after all."

"Frankly, I don't see how we're going to do it either," Amanda admitted. "If someone's taking money out of your account, they're certainly not going to *tell* us their code. But don't call that meeting just yet. Maybe we'll think of something. I'm going to run my program during study hall. Then I have dance practice; so I'll see you later at home."

"Okay," said Sherlock, "but I hope you'll have thought of something by then. I've got to find that money soon."

This time Amanda's program ran smoothly. After dance practice, she waited impatiently for her friend Sylvia Blum to finish getting dressed. "I'll meet you in front of the bulletin board," she said finally. "I don't see how you can spend so much time combing your hair."

Amanda tapped hor foot and started reading through the notices posted on the board.

"I'm ready, Amanda," Sylvia called cheerfully. She was hurrying down the hall, her blond hair perfectly flipped back.

"Oh, Sylvia," said Amanda, startled. "I was reading about all these club trips, and I completely forgot about you. Let's go."

"Where were you?" Sherlock asked, when Amanda finally got home. "I've been waiting for hours. Jack Wharton came up to me after math class to tell me how excited he is about the trip. I felt terrible."

"I was waiting for Sylvia," Amanda explained. "She takes longer to get ready than anyone I know. My program ran perfectly, though."

"Terrific," said Sherlock, "but have you got any ideas about *my* problem?"

"I'm not sure," she replied. "I have an idea, but I don't want to say anything until I've checked it further. The first thing I have to do is take another look at that piece of printout that was attached to my program yesterday. Remember? It looked like a payment record."

"Sure, I remember," Sherlock said. "But it didn't have a code on it."

"I know," Amanda answered mysteriously, going off to her room.

The next morning she hurried Sherlock through breakfast. "Come on, I want to look something up in the library before class. If I'm right, you'll have your money back in time for your road trip."

"Good morning," Amanda greeted the librarian politely, while Sherlock trailed after her. "Could you please tell me where the chess books are kept?"

"Good morning, Amanda and Sherlock. You're both here very early. Second shelf of the third bookcase on your left, Amanda."

"Thank you," said Amanda as they both hurried down the aisle.

She pulled one book after another off the shelf until she found the one she was looking for. Then she triumphantly held the page open in front of Sherlock. "There! Now I think we'd better go find Tommy Wolfe and see about getting your money back."

**The solution to this mystery is on page 42.**

# BOOM TO BOOM

"Congratulations," said Sherlock.

"To whom?" Amanda asked.

"To me, for my expert handling of this boat," he answered, grinning. "You can call me Captain from now on." Just then, a sudden change in wind swung the boom around and knocked Sherlock into the bay.

"Are you all right, Captain?" Amanda called over the side of the boat.

"Very funny," Sherlock yelled back. He was bobbing up and down in his orange life jacket.

"Hold on, I'll pick you up."

"No! Take the boat in. I'll swim.... Meet you at the dock."

Ten minutes later, Sherlock pulled himself ashore, stripped off the life jacket, and sat down on the sand to collect himself.

He rubbed a bump on the back of his head. After a few minutes, he picked himself up and started down the beach in the direction of the dock, his head bent in search of more beach glass for his collection. He was concentrating so hard that he almost walked right into Mr. Nelson, who owned the bait store on the dock.

The old man was sitting , with his back turned, but as soon as he heard Sherlock approach, he swung around and started screaming.

"What are you doing sneaking up on me like that? What are you staring at?"

"Who, me?" Sherlock asked, surprised by the outburst. He glanced behind him to see if Mr. Nelson was yelling at someone else. "I didn't sneak up...." Before Sherlock could finish his sentence, he was stunned by a blow on the head. The next thing he knew, he was waking up on a cot in a dingy room cluttered with an amazing collection of junk.

He sat up and felt his head. Now there were two bumps, symmetrically placed, one near each ear. Sherlock was trying to imagine what he would look like with a pair of horns, when he heard a key turn in the lock. The door opened, and Mr. Nelson stood glaring at him.

"Where am I?" asked Sherlock.

"None of your business," was Mr. Nelson's answer.

"But why did you hit me? How long have I been here? I'm supposed to meet my sister at the dock."

"Sorry," Mr. Nelson replied, "but you're going to have to stay here awhile. I can't let you go; not after what you saw."

"But I didn't see anything," Sherlock protested. "I don't know what you're talking about."

Mr. Nelson obviously didn't believe him. "Sorry, kid, but I know you saw me burying those explosives. I let you go, and you'll just mess up all my plans."

With that the old man stomped out and locked the door behind him.

Sherlock was alone again in the windowless room. A small shaft of light from a crack in the wall allowed him to examine the contents of his new quarters. In addition to the cot, there were boxes of old clothing, hardware, fishing gear, boat parts, and broken furniture.

Somehow, he would have to think of a way to get a message to Amanda.

At first Amanda was worried. She'd waited on the dock and Sherlock had never shown up. When she found his life jacket on the beach, she had stopped worrying and got angry instead. Probably he'd wandered off looking for more beach glass and forgotten all about their meeting. But when night came, and he still hadn't returned, Mr. and Mrs. Jones insisted on calling the police.

Sherlock had just finished collecting the items he needed to leave a message, and had left them by the door in an old canvas bait bag, when Mr. Nelson came back with a glass of milk and a doughnut.

"Here, eat this," he growled, "then I got a job for you to do."

"Sure," said Sherlock, "whatever you say, and thanks for the food."

When he'd finished eating, Mr. Nelson took the empty plate and glass and, without another word, tied a fishy smelling old rag around Sherlock's eyes.

"Hey, wait a minute, what are you doing?" Sherlock protested.

"Sorry, kid, gotta do this," the old man replied. He took Sherlock's arm and started walking.

Sherlock's foot hit the bait bag, and he grabbed it on the way out the door. They walked on the sand, in what seemed like a huge circle, then up three steps.

Mr. Nelson stopped short, and abruptly removed the blindfold. They were standing in front of the bait store and the night was pitch black.

"Take this," he said, thrusting a square of white paper at Sherlock. "Put it up on that board over there, and then you come right back. No funny business. Don't try running off to warn them people at the power plant."

Sherlock could see a sharp bait knife hanging from Mr. Nelson's belt. "Right." He nodded vigorously and ran toward the bulletin board at the end of the dock. He went around to the side facing the bay and pinned up the sign. THREE DAYS TIL THE LIGHTS GO OUT, he read in the dim light from a passing boat. Then, quickly, he dropped three items out of the bait bag and hurried back to Mr. Nelson, who blindfolded him again and led him back the way they'd come.

When Sherlock still wasn't home the next morning, Amanda decided it was time to do some searching on her own. She'd start at the dock, which was where he should have been when he disappeared.

"Hi, Sam," she greeted the captain of the local charter boat. "You haven't seen my brother, Sherlock, around, have you?"

"Sorry, Amanda," he replied. "Seems like I haven't seen him for a couple of days."

And no one else had seen him either. Amanda sat down on a bench near the bulletin board at the dock to think. Staring idly at the signs offering bicycles for sale and baby-sitting services, she noticed the white square of paper with the strange warning, then the three odd items lying beneath it. Curious, she picked them up — a dirty, green T shirt, a broken lobster trap, and a rusty old padlock. She sat down on the ground and laid them out in front of her. She moved them around. She wrinkled her forehead in concentration, and then, abruptly, she realized Sherlock was sending her a message.

When he had found himself on the dock, Sherlock got a pretty good idea of where he was being kept, but it was so dark he couldn't be absolutely certain. Before going to sleep, he collected three more items for the bait bag.

When Mr. Nelson came in with his breakfast the next morning — another doughnut and more milk — Sherlock was ready.

"Listen," he started in, trying to sound as reasonable as possible, "people are going to be looking for me. You'd better let me go, or else you're really going to be in trouble."

"In trouble already," Mr. Nelson answered. "Can't let them get my land. Can't let you stop me."

It was a long, boring day, with nothing to do but think up impossible escape plans. That night, however, when the angry old man once more led him around to the dock, Sherlock was certain he knew the location of the dingy room. He was also pleased to discover that the first three items were no longer where he'd left them. Perhaps Amanda had found them after all.

Amanda had hung around the dock until it got dark, questioning everyone she saw. Then she reluctantly gathered up the objects she knew had been left by Sherlock and headed for home. But she was back first thing the next morning, and sure enough there were three more items left in the same place. The message on

the bulletin board had also been changed, and this one was much more frightening. TWO DAYS. THE SITUATION IS EXPLOSIVE, it said. Amanda didn't wait any longer. She picked up the plant mister, the box of nails, and the empty bottle of suntan oil, and went off to figure out the code.

Once Sherlock knew where he was, he hunted carefully through the junk-filled room, climbing over cartons and tossing aside one thing after another, to find just the right clues for Amanda.

The next morning, Mr. Nelson seemed angrier than ever.

"What's the matter?" Sherlock asked. "Have people been looking for me?"

"Fools won't listen to me. One more warning, and then I'm really gonna do it," Mr. Nelson growled and stormed out.

"So, tonight's my last chance," Sherlock thought gloomily. "This had better work."

Amanda was so excited she could hardly sleep that night. She was sure there would be another message in the morning, and that it would give her the final piece of information she'd need to find Sherlock. When she got to the dock, she saw that the new warning on the

bulletin board was even more explicit than the last. TOWN COUNCIL BEWARE: IT'S BIG BOOM TOMORROW. Amanda sat down to examine the clues. Once more she started moving things around, lining them up and muttering under her breath. It was only a few minutes before she had the answer. Then, grabbing the evidence, she rushed off in search of help to rescue Sherlock.

**The solution to this mystery is on page 44 .**

# HOME RUN SABOTAGE

The pitch was high and outside, but the batter swung at it just the same and connected with a sound that everyone knew meant a home run.

"Did you see that?" Sherlock screamed at his sister.

"Yeah, it's a home run," said Amanda, not turning to look at her brother. Her eyes were glued to the field.

"No," said Sherlock. "Not the home run. Did you see how he pulled that ball?"

"Pulled what? He hit it with his bat," she answered.

Amanda watched Billy Fox round the bases. Three years ago, he had been a star in the world series, driving in winning runs. Now, after two consecutive seasons in a batting slump, he was back in the minors. The home run didn't seem to lift his spirits, and he took the bases with a disinterested stride, ignoring the crowd as they cheered.

"I'm glad I'm not interviewing *him*," said Amanda, her eyes still intent on the field.

"Well, Tommy Wingfield doesn't look like such a great candidate for your interview either," said Sherlock.

Having struck out the first three batters in the first inning, Wingfield, the pitcher, was angry at giving up this run. He kicked up the dirt on the mound, sending dust clouds all over the infield. This was Wingfield's last game in the minors and he wanted it to be a good one.

After the game, Amanda was going to interview Tommy Wingfield for the school newspaper. His career in the major leagues was about to begin, just as it seemed that Billy Fox's was ending.

"He looks so big out there on the mound. It's hard to believe he ever went to our school," said Amanda.

"He sure is good, though," said Sherlock. "Look at him fire that fast ball."

"Steee-rike threeee!" the umpire called.

Wingfield retired the side, and at the end of the second inning the score was one/nothing.

Amanda's need to feel prepared for the interview filled her with a million questions and a brand-new interest in a game she had always thought was boring.

"Let's go get a hot dog," Sherlock suggested.

"You go. I'm staying right here until this game is over," said Amanda. "But first, what are all those signs and signals everyone is making — the coach to the base runner, the pitcher to the catcher, the catcher to the pitcher?"

"Well, each team develops its own set of hand signs to signal among themselves without the other team knowing," Sherlock said. "It's like a secret code. The coach tells the base runner when to run. The catcher, who plays in every game and gets to know all the hitters, tells the pitcher what to throw, and the pitcher will either okay the catcher's call, or ask for another pitch. It's important for the catcher to know what's coming, so he'll know how to play it.... I'll be back with my hot dog in a minute," Sherlock said.

Amanda turned back to the game just in time to see the third baseman on Wingfield's team smack a long, high ball deep into right field for a triple.

At the top of the sixth inning, the score was all tied up at two/two. In spite of a surprise double by Wingfield, the visiting team went down without bringing in a run.

"Fox will be up again this inning," said Sherlock. "Maybe he'll hit a tie-breaking homer — like he used to in the majors."

"Maybe," said Amanda, and she turned her attention back to the game as the first man up for the home team hit a hard line drive to left field, pulling up safe at first. Fox swung two bats over his head, threw one down, and stepped up to the plate. The catcher, Sam Bowles, a retired major leaguer and former teammate of Fox's, called for the pitch. Wingfield threw one high and outside, and the smack of a solid hit echoed through the park. It looked like a certain home run, but Amanda and Sherlock sank back into their seats as the ball went foul. The catcher signaled again, but Wingfield shook

his head and gave the sign for a fast ball. He fired a bullet, dead center over the plate. A swing and a miss; strike two.

Bowles tore off his face mask and marched up to the mound.

"That pitch looked good to me," Sherlock said. "What are they arguing about?"

The catcher finally settled into his crouch back at the plate and signaled for the next pitch. Wingfield hesitated, then let go with the ball. Fox connected again, and the ball whizzed past the shortstop. Fox was on base. Two men on and no one out. For the moment, it looked good for the home team. Wingfield, however,

was determined not to let them score. The next man up popped out to center, and the following two went down swinging. The side was retired, leaving two men stranded.

"Who do you want to win the game?" Sherlock asked Amanda.

"I don't know who to root for anymore," she answered.

Both pitchers began to lose their control in a very active eighth inning. There were singles and doubles and walks for both sides, but neither team added to the score. In the top of the ninth, the visitors went down in order, and the home team was now up to try to break the tie and win the game. The fans moaned, watching the first two men strike out, but the third man up connected for a solid line drive and a base hit.

"Here he comes!" Sherlock yelled as Fox walked up to the batter's box.

"I've got my fingers crossed," Amanda yelled back, perched on the edge of her seat.

Bowles made his call and Wingfield fired off a perfect fast ball. A swing and a miss; strike one. The next pitch was high and inside — Fox let it go for a ball.

"One and one, right?" Amanda asked. Sherlock nodded without taking his eyes off the field.

The catcher signaled again. Following Bowles's call, Wingfield threw a bad pitch and waited for the umpire to call ball two. But Fox went after it and connected. The ball sailed over the fence for the winning home run.

The game was over. Amanda and Sherlock were on their feet screaming as Wingfield threw down his glove and stomped off the field.

"What do you say to someone who's just lost his last game in the minors, even if he is on his way to a major league club?" Amanda asked Sherlock.

"I don't know. Why don't you ask him about his double in the top of the sixth?" Sherlock suggested, as they followed the signs to the visiting team's office.

The door to the office was open, but no one was there when they arrived. Amanda and Sherlock walked in and sat down to wait for Tommy Wingfield.

"Hey, Amanda!" said Sherlock, eyeing a blackboard
in the corner. But just then the losing pitcher walked in.
"That was quite some hit you had in the sixth inning,"
said Amanda with a big smile.

"Yes," Wingfield answered politely. "But that's not what a pitcher is there for."

"I guess you're right," Amanda answered. "How would you account for the outcome of today's game?"

"I don't know," Wingfield answered, shaking his head. "Fox was certainly hot today, but I can't understand why Sam kept asking for those pitches. When I tried to question him, I thought he'd bite my head off."

Amanda looked at Sherlock and abruptly ended the interview.

"Thank you very much," she said. "You've been very helpful."

"Is that it?" asked the surprised pitcher.

"We've got everything we need," said Sherlock, as he and Amanda dashed out the door. "Good luck in the majors!"

"Quick," Amanda said. "Maybe we can catch Fox as he comes out of the clubhouse."

"Mr. Fox!" Amanda called as they spotted the star of the day heading toward his car. "Can I ask you a few questions for my school newspaper?"

Fox, looking happier than he had during the early part of the game, nodded and waited for them to catch up. After introducing themselves, Amanda fired off as many questions as she could think of.

"It sure feels good to be hitting again," Fox said, getting into his white convertible. "But, you know, it's almost as though Wingfield knew what balls I liked and threw them to me on purpose — as if he *wanted* me to hit them."

"Well, not quite," Amanda said to Sherlock as Fox pulled out of the parking lot. "But somebody certainly did."

**The solution to this mystery is on page 46.**

# THE
# SOLUTIONS

# COMPUTER OVERBYTE

## The Solution

Sherlock's Athletic Club funds are being embezzled by Tommy Wolfe, whose Chess Club is short of funds and who must find the money to pay for their three-day tournament in Springfield. Tommy has learned Sherlock's computer code and has used it to gain access to his electronic-transfer account.

## The Code

Each user of the computer has a log-on code that allows them access to the terminal, and that also protects their program from use by anyone else. Amanda's code is AMA. Sherlock's is LOCK. Amanda and Sherlock realize that the embezzler's code is P-K4, but they must find out who it belongs to. The answer lies in the chess book, which shows that P-K4 is an abbreviation for the traditional opening move, Pawn to King four.

*Here are the clues Amanda and Sherlock used to solve the mystery:*

Page 7

The last page of someone else's program is attached to a page of Amanda's printout. Amanda's page shows her log-on code, AMA, at the top, but the previous program has no code because the first page is missing. It does, however, show payments to a bus company, and to a hotel in Springfield for three nights. The total is $98.95.

When Sherlock goes to make his Athletic Club payments, he discovers that there is only thirty-five dollars in his account — substantially less than there should have been. He checks his written records and confirms that he should have had a balance of $135.27.

As they pass the room where the Chess

Club is meeting, Sherlock comments that they have had a hard time raising money during the year.

Sherlock checks the computer records against his own. The display on the monitor shows:

LOG-ON ACCEPTED FOR LOCK 8:02

PAYMENT TO BEST UNIFORM CO. — $ 32.50

DEPOSIT                                             50.00

PAYMENT TO ALLIED SPORTING
GOODS                                               26.25

TRANSFER OUT TO ACCOUNT P-K4     100.00

Thinking that the code — P-K4 — might represent someone's initials, Amanda and Sherlock check the computer class list, but that proves to be a dead end. Amanda stops to read announcements on the bulletin board, including that of Sherlock's Athletic Club trip, and a three-day tournament the Chess Club will be playing in Springfield against the Benjamin Franklin School.

When Amanda checks the printout, she sees a payment to a hotel in Springfield, and also that the amount paid out is almost exactly the same as the amount missing from the Athletic Club account.

The chess book Amanda finds in the library shows sample games laid out with the abbreviations traditionally used to indicate moves in chess. The one Amanda points out to Sherlock is P-K4.

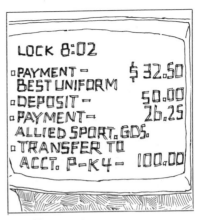

Page 11

Page 14

Page 16

# BOOM TO BOOM

## The Solution

Sherlock is being held prisoner in the unused shed behind Mr. Nelson's bait store because he has accidentally stumbled upon the old man burying explosives in the sand. Reading the warning notes, and listening to the old man's complaints, Sherlock realizes that Mr. Nelson plans to blow up the power plant, which, with the agreement of the Town Council, is about to take over his land in order to expand their facilities.

## The Code

Sherlock realizes that if he can leave certain objects for Amanda to find, they will provide clues to his predicament. The three items left each day, when arranged in the proper order, form rebuses that eventually lead Amanda to the bait store.

*Here are the clues Amanda and Sherlock used to solve the mystery:*

When Sherlock sees Mr. Nelson on the beach, the old man's back is turned, so that Sherlock can't see what he's doing. Nelson, however, doesn't realize this and believes Sherlock has seen him burying the explosives.

Sherlock examines the contents of the room in which he is trapped. Among the junk are all the items he later leaves as clues for Amanda.

Though blindfolded, Sherlock knows he is being led through sand, around in a circle,

Page 20

and up some steps. When he finds himself on the dock in front of the bait store, he begins to figure out that he's being held as a prisoner in the shed behind the store. Sherlock also has a chance to read the first warning message he's put up for Mr. Nelson — a cryptic reference to the power plant.

Amanda finds the first three items left by Sherlock, and moves them around until finally she realizes that the objects form a re-bus: *Sherlock is trapped.*

The next morning, Sherlock learns from his conversation with Mr. Nelson that someone is trying to take Mr. Nelson's land away.

Sherlock leaves his second set of clues which, when discovered by Amanda, provides her with the name of Sherlock's captor: *Mr. Nelson.*

At the same time, Amanda reads the second warning, with its ominous reference to explosives.

The next morning, Amanda discovers the third and final warning, which refers to the Town Council.

The items that Sherlock has left lead Amanda to Sherlock's location. She correctly interprets the last three objects to mean: *Bait Store, Dock.*

Page 20

Page 23

Page 25

Page 27

# HOME RUN SABOTAGE

## The Solution

It wasn't until the following year that Amanda was able to complete her interview with Tommy Wingfield. Now "Rookie of the Year," Wingfield listened as Amanda explained the mystery of his last game in the minors. She told him how he was tricked by Bowles into throwing the pitches that Fox hit best. Bowles, Amanda explained, had taken Fox under his wing when they were teammates in the majors. Now permanently retired from major league play, the old catcher wanted to help Fox fight his way out of his slump and back to the majors, where he belonged.

## The Code

Bowles uses hand signals to tell the pitcher what to throw. Whenever Fox comes up to bat, he asks for pitches that were outside. Later, while Amanda and Sherlock were in the office waiting for Wingfield, Sherlock saw the team's codes for the day written on the blackboard. He was able to put together the written code with the signals he has seen Sam Bowles giving earlier, and with the pitches Billy Fox had been hitting so successfully.

*Here are the clues Amanda and Sherlock used to solve the mystery:*

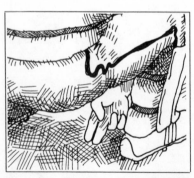

Page 32

The first home run that Fox hits is on a pitch that is high and outside. Sherlock comments on the "pulled ball" — something that Fox had a reputation for when he played major league ball.

Sherlock explains to Amanda how hand signals are used by the players to communicate among themselves.

In the sixth inning, the catcher signals for a ball that is high and outside — the same kind of ball that Fox hit for his home run in the second inning. He almost does it again, but the ball goes foul at the last minute. On the next pitch, Wingfield annoys Bowles by questioning his call for a high, outside ball. Sherlock can't understand why the catcher is arguing, after Wingfield has thrown a strike.

Page 34

Bowles signals again for another high, outside pitch. Wingfield hesitates, but this time he doesn't argue, and again Fox connects.

The next time Fox comes up to bat, Bowles changes his tactics to keep Wingfield from becoming suspicious. He calls first for a fast ball, next for a high inside pitch. Then he signals for a pitch that is low and outside. Sure enough, Fox connects for a home run that wins the game.

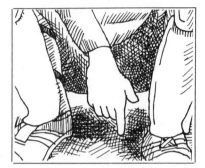
Page 36

Seeing the blackboard with the visiting team's signals written on it, Sherlock recalls the hand signs Bowles used during the game. There was no doubt about it. Bowles had been calling for the outside pitches Fox was famous for hitting so well in the majors.

When Wingfield says he can't understand why Bowles called for pitches that seemed easy for Fox to hit, Amanda comes up with the same conclusion as Sherlock. They run to interview Fox as well.

Fox's admission that he's been thrown his favorite kinds of pitches absolutely convinces them that although Bowles is a catcher, he was throwing the game.

HIGH OUTSIDE

LOW OUTSIDE

Page 38

**HIDDEN CLUE BOOKS**

**MYSTERIES**
**THE HOUSE ON BLACKTHORN HILL**
**FLUTE REVENGE**

**CODEBREAKERS**
**RUBIK'S RUSE**
**COMPUTER OVERBYTE**